WARNING

This book contains sexually explicit scenes and adult language. It may be considered offensive to some readers. This book is for sale to adults ONLY.

* * * * * * * * * * * * * * * * * *

Please store your files wisely where they cannot be accessed by underage readers.

ISBN-13: 978-1987863840
ISBN-10: 1987863844

Other Books by Darla Dunbar:

<u>The Romeo Alpha BBW Paranormal Shifter Romance Series</u>

Amanda Walker thinks that she has a normal and boring life. That is until after her 24th birthday. Everything changes when she meets the man who says he was supposed to be her husband. Denying everything the man says, she fights him every step of the way. But after he kidnaps her, Amanda discovers that there are some things about her family that her parents kept a secret all these years. Among the history of the family she learns secrets she thought only happened in story books. Can Amanda tell the difference between truth and lies or is she this mysterious woman that holds the key to a legacy?

<u>Romeo Alpha Blood Lines Romance Series</u>

Twenty-four years have passed in relative peace for Amanda and Romeo. They've raised five children into adulthood and are thoroughly enjoying their lives as the Alpha King and Queen of the werewolves. At twenty-four, Sarina is just stepping into her powers and will be ripe for mating when her birthday comes in two weeks. What no one knows is the danger that lurks just outside their tight knit community. Romeo has made peace with the other clans and has enjoyed that peace, but it will all come crashing down around him when his oldest daughter comes of age to take a mate.

The Alpha Feud BBW Paranormal Shifter Romance Series

Eliza's life consisted of reporting on boring, crowd-pleasing events, like their country livestock fair. With the arrival of two handsome brothers, the lives of Eliza and her best friend, Melissa, are shaken to the core. For Eliza, the arrival of this new man becomes a test of her relationship with her current boyfriend, who she's been happily living with for over six years. Does Hayden, a complete stranger, really wield the power to make Eliza reconsider her relationship with Andrew?

The Alpha Packed BBW Paranormal Shifter Romance Series

Darlene has led a quiet life since suffering through a terrible break-up. She wants nothing more than to spend her time in front of the TV, away from any sort of trouble. But all that goes down the drain when handsome, rugged and rough Idris comes into her life. He is a werewolf on the lookout for his missing pack leader. Darlene quickly finds herself pulled towards this mysterious man and at the same time finds herself falling deeper and deeper into the world of the supernatural.

The Mind Talker Paranormal Romance Series

Ananda finds herself on the run and she's not alone. With help from Jared, a stranger that she just met, the two evade capture by an organization that is intent on hunting her kind. Ananda and Jared are able to read minds. When an unfortunate incident happened involving a disturbed individual that resulted in the death of his schoolmates, the secret organization decided to take action.

<u>The Leather Satchel Paranormal Romance Series</u>

Valtina is stuck in Middle World, unable to pass on to The Afterlife. In order to redeem herself from past deeds done, she must help bring romance back into the world and stop The Dark Side from destroying love in its entirety. Following orders issued by Ladaya and armed with a leather satchel filled with the appropriate tools and weapons, Valtina embraces each mission with enthusiasm.

Get the latest update on new releases from the author at:

https://darladunbar.com/newsletter/

This book is Part Four of "<u>The Daemon Paranormal Romance Chronicles</u>"

Book 1 - The Awakening

Phoebe grew up not knowing her mother. The stranger, Apollo Mikos, claimed to know her mother. After that day, Phoebe's life would change forever.

Book 2 - The Shifter

Phoebe is surprised when her dog, Ace, shows up from nowhere. She is on a mission with Apollo to kill the Qilin. That is the only way that the true leader of daemons will emerge.

Book 3 - Forgotten

Juno has been stirring up trouble that has prolonged the infighting among the daemons. In order to get her to stop, Phoebe agrees to give up a year of her memories. But making deals with a siren is never a good thing. Without her memories, Phoebe's romantic relationship with Supay no longer exists. Instead, she leaves Supay for Apollo.

Book 4 - The Siren's Trap

The unsuspecting couple, Phoebe and Supay, made a deal with Juno to stop the infighting among the daemons. But at what price? An entire year was wiped clean from Phoebe's mind. Now Phoebe was with Apollo. Desperate to get her back, Supay considers Juno's new deal. Is it worth the price to pay for the dubious result? To win back Phoebe's love, Supay will need to be unfaithful to her.

Book 5 - Exposed

Hiding away in Peru, Supay and Phoebe start their own family, away from the chaos and the daemon infighting. Meanwhile, Apollo, heart-broken and lost, is lured into another one of Juno's schemes. Making deals with a siren never turns out right. If Apollo accepts the deal, the love of his life may resent him for the rest of his natural life. If he doesn't take the deal, she is lost to him forever.

Book 6 - The Beginning

As preparations for the war between daemons are underway, everyone must begin to choose. Siding temporarily with Apollo, Juno has a moment to look back on her life and figure out how she arrived at this moment. As she sifts through memories of the past, a specific dark stranger stands out. How far will young Juno go with her new love? More importantly, will her mother, Circe, discover the secret tryst?

Book 7 - The Treachery

Having broken the cardinal rule of the sirens, Juno must take action to save her own life and the life of her unborn child. In order to keep her secret safe from the sisterhood, she must kill her lover and conceal her shame. Will Juno betray the sisterhood and save her lover or will she remain loyal by slaying him instead?

Book 8 - Duplicity

Juno's mother, Circe, discovers her lies and gives her an ultimatum to fix everything. As Juno races against the clock to protect her loved ones from Circe, she makes a final choice that could leave her perpetually unhappy. Left to wander the world alone, Juno realizes that freedom means nothing if there is no one to share it with. The nature of Juno's vendetta—and the means she achieves it with—are finally revealed.

Book 9 - Reconnaissance

As Juno's hunt for the daemon's fortress unfolds, Apollo is left alone wondering if she will truly return to him. Will Juno be able to resist her base instincts? More importantly, will she be able to get to the fortress and return without being spotted? Discover how Juno's stealth mission works out.

Book 10 - The Interrogation

Juno tries to hide her rising fear in the presence of her captors. As her fear mounts, she holds on to the hope that Phoebe or Supay will take pity on her. Before that can happen, she has to come clean to Supay about her past. Could he possibly forgive her for what she has done? Will Juno remain faithful to Apollo or will her siren urges take over? Discover how the confrontation with Supay unfolds.

The Daemon Paranormal Romance Chronicles

The Siren's Trap

Book Four

By Darla Dunbar

Copyright Revelry Publishing 2015

Table of Contents

Chapter One

PHOEBE STARED out at the ocean. In La Coruna, or A Coruna as the locals called it, the ocean was everything. Next to her was the world's oldest lighthouse. It was said to have been built by Hercules himself in ancient times. After several weeks of being in Spain and an excellent grammar book, she was finally starting to pick up on the language. Right now was not the time for studying. This moment was hers alone to stare into the great expanse of ocean before her. Across those waters, she had helped to search for a new leader, find the Qilin, and fell in love.

Already, memories were starting to float back into her mind. The spiteful witch, Juno, had taken her memories temporarily. As memories of Supay started to flow back, Phoebe realized why. Juno was not intent on leading daemons to take over the world or even gain power. They had overestimated her goals. From everything that Phoebe could figure out, Juno just wanted to cause trouble. She thrived on causing hurt to people. Although Juno had agreed to stay out of the infighting, she had managed to split Supay and Phoebe apart. Now, Phoebe was across the world with Apollo. He had rented a condo near the beach and spent each day trying to prove his love. At first, his attempts had been endearing. Now, it felt like he was smothering her.

In reality, nothing may have been different. She had just started to change as her memories came back. Phoebe remembered Supay's cute quirks and his dedication to always doing what was right. She also remembered her own disapproval of Apollo and his intention to kill the Qilin. Alone at the edge of the world, there was no escape from her memories.

Picking her way down the rocks, Phoebe got as close to the ocean as possible. The few tourists that were there spoke Spanish, since La Coruna was a Spanish-tourist destination. On occasion, she ran into the random English family who had decided to take holiday there. The number of English speakers that she had met could be counted on one hand. It made for a lonely existence, but she felt less alone as her Spanish improved. The warmth of Spain and the salty sea air were a welcome change from the thin air at Cuzco.

Sitting down on a rock, Phoebe started to cry. Since finding out she was pregnant, her hormones had gone haywire. It did not help that she truly was in a bad situation. She was stuck in Spain with Apollo and could not bring herself to tell him that she was pregnant. Since she was only a few months along, it still was not noticeable. Even worse, she could not bring herself to call Supay and tell him that she was going to have their child. Unless Supay stopped by the cabin, he may not even know that she was gone. Even worse, he may have already realized she was gone. If so, he would be frantic with worry.

Drying her tears, Phoebe stood shakily up. The wind was starting to get chilly as the sun set.

Wandering back to the condo, she put on a smile as she walked through the door. Like normal, Apollo saw what he wanted to see. If she seemed happy, he was not going to question it. Walking up to her, he gave her a kiss.

"Did you enjoy your walk?" he asked. He turned to the stove and continued to sauté some vegetables for dinner.

"Yes, it really is beautiful out here," she answered and turned to set the table. "What are you up to today?"

"Not much. I was just reading through some e-mails about the daemon problems. Although the fighting is still going on, there haven't been any deaths for at least a few weeks." He placed the vegetables on the place and pulled out a baguette. Looking in the oven, he removed a tray of lasagna.

Putting the food on her plate, Phoebe started to eat. She forgot for a moment to guard her expression and her sadness crept in. Noticing the change in expression, Apollo looked at her in confusion.

"What's wrong?" he asked. "Are you starting to get your memories back yet?" He appeared worried. Apollo knew that there was a chance she would leave him when her memories returned.

Phoebe shrugged. "Some memories have come back. Don't worry, I'm still here." She paused and tried to frame her thoughts. "I was thinking today... maybe I should call Supay. From what I remember, it wouldn't really be fair to just run off without telling him where I am. If he has already realized that I am gone, he is probably freaking out right now."

Apollo pressed his lips into a thin line. Moving forward to pick up her place, he kissed her. "If you think that is what's best."

Biting her lip, Phoebe shrugged in response. "Best for me or you? I really don't know the answer. But letting him know that I am alive seems like the right thing to do."

Leaving the room, she sat down at the computer. Already, she was worrying about what to say. An e-mail would be far easier to type up than a phone call. She did not want to hear the pain or disappointment in his voice.

Sitting down, she started to type: "It's me, Supay. If you went to the cabin, you probably already know that I am gone. I couldn't take not knowing my past or just waiting to remember. From what I remember, I loved Apollo once. I ran into him in town and we started traveling together. Don't worry about me, I am safe."

Staring at it, the letter sounded so heartless. Although she wanted to soften it, she knew it would not help. She wanted the e-mail to show that she was not returning to him and that he could not be with her. If she softened it at all, it would only give him hope. Before she could change her mind, she clicked send and sat back. She had done her part. For some reason, she still felt so awful. Walking into the bedroom, she saw Apollo naked on the bed. Next to him, he had a whip, a blindfold, and restraints. Sex had become more adventurous in the last few weeks. They had spent each evening pushing each other to the limit of pleasure and pain. Although she doubted other people would understand their sexual desires, it did not matter to her.

Smiling wickedly, Phoebe's mood brightened instantly. "Am I the dominatrix today? Or are you going to take your turn as master?"

Apollo stretched back and rested his head on his hands. When he did that, it caused each muscle in his chest and arms to pop out. With his best submissive face, he motioned toward the whip. "I'm all yours, mistress."

Nodding, Phoebe picked up the ropes and made him sit in the chair. She tied his hands behind the chair and placed a gag over his mouth.

"While I prepare, you can wait patiently for me. I want you to spend the next hour thinking about what you could be doing with me." She stripped out of her clothes and watched his eyes follow each movement of her body. Running her hand along her body, she let his desire and arousal increase. Walking to the closet, she put on a pair of black stilettos. Naked, she stood in front of the mirror in them. Her legs looked impossibly long and gorgeous in the shoes. The stilettos caused her thigh muscles and butt to tighten. Admiring herself for a moment, she noticed a tiny, imperceptible pouch on her stomach. Frowning slightly, she glanced over at Apollo. He still did not notice anything was different about her body.

Going back into the closet, she found a black corset and lacy black underwear. Putting them on, she pulled out her makeup and sat at the vanity. Apollo continued to watch each move she made. She ran her hand from her stilettos up to the parting of her thighs. Touching herself briefly, she made eye contact with Apollo and smiled. She could tease him all night and still want more. Pulling out her makeup, she slowly prepared herself. As a final touch, she added bright red lipstick and pulled on black gloves.

Turning back to Apollo, she snapped the whip. The sound resounded in her ears. Flicking on her iPod, she turned on music to drown out any sounds the neighbors might hear. Reaching her arm back, the whip whistled through the air until it made contact with his thigh. Wincing, he kept from crying out. She whipped him again for wincing. He waited for another whipping, but she stopped and traced the tips of the whip along his body. The pleasurable feeling was even more enjoyable after the pain of just a few seconds ago. As she ran the whip across his shoulders, he shivered in pleasure. Noticing his enjoyment, Phoebe told him to wait. Leaving the room, she went to the kitchen and filled a cup with ice.

She returned to the room and set the cup of ice on the night table. Kneeling down in front of him, she took him into her mouth. Unable to stop himself, Apollo groaned with desire. He pushed his hips upwards so that she would take the whole shaft into her mouth. Pulling back, Phoebe looked at him in mock anger.

"If you recall, I am the mistress. Understood?" she asked.

He nodded.

"Yes, what?" she demanded.

"Yes, mistress," he mumbled through the gag.

As punishment, she took a piece of ice into her hand and started to trace it along his body. She stopped at his nipples. The cold hardened his nipples and was almost unbearable. Putting the ice cube in her mouth, she went down on him. As much as he wanted her to go down on him, the shape of the cube felt uncomfortable against him. He could have born the cold, but the additional space usage made it so that there was no room for him in her mouth. Moaning in frustration, Apollo could not bear the agony of waiting any more.

Glancing up, Phoebe realized that she had pushed him to the limit of waiting. Untying his arms, she let him become free of the constraints. Without waiting for her to say anything, he threw her onto the bed. She landed on her bottom and waited. The lack of action teased him even more. Pulling back her hair, he pushed her mouth onto his cock. Moving her head back and forth, Apollo leaned back and moaned in pleasure. Finally, he was getting his satisfaction after such a long wait for her.

He watched her go down on him for a moment longer and then pushed her back completely onto the bed. Spreading her legs, he grasped her lacy underwear in his teeth. Above him, her breasts popped out of her corset, too large to be constrained by the garment any more. Ripping her underwear off, he positioned himself in front of her. He rubbed the tip of his head against her clit. After all of her teasing, she was going to be punished. Phoebe rocked her hips in anticipation, but nothing happened. Apollo stroked himself while she watched and waited. When he touched his cock against her again, she took action. Wrapping her legs around his bottom, she pulled him into her tightly and did not let go. Once inside, the wetness and creaminess enticed Apollo to continue. Animal desire overcame his yearning to tease her. Pushing into her, he was already close to orgasm. Taking deep breaths, he tried to stave off the inevitable. Seeing how close he was, Phoebe clenched her muscles tightly around his cock. As she clenched and unclenched, it drove him wild with longing. He could not hold back any longer. Putting the entire weight of his body onto her, he thrust with a wild abandon. Nothing existed in the world except for him and Phoebe. Unable to control himself any longer, he came into her. Gasping, Phoebe started to orgasm at the same time. The hours spent in anticipation heightened her orgasm to a level she had never reached before. Dimly, she wondered at the back of her mind if this is what the monks tried to seek in enlightenment. Drugged by desire and sex, she rolled over and into Apollo's arms.

Chapter Two

Across the world, Supay sat alone in a bar. A nondescript pub, the customers around him seemed to be distracted by their personal problems. Ordering another drink, he wandered over to the old-school jukebox that sat in the corner and started to search for a song. A voice behind him suddenly caught his attention.

"Well, well, well. If it isn't Supay. Are you depressed that your sweet princess is in the arms of another man?" The musical tinkling voice behind him could only be Juno. Sighing in exasperation, he turned around.

"Don't you have someone else to bother?" He glared at her. Juno's meddling was the reason Phoebe was gone. If there was ever a real-life femme fatale, it was Juno.

She smiled seductively and leaned against the jukebox. Her breasts rose slightly with each breath, and Supay could see down her shirt. Remembering the few dates they had gone on, he could not help thinking about her naked. Annoyed at himself for thinking about that, he turned to her.

"Well, my ancestors were sirens. What do you think? I'm pretty certain that it is my job to lure people toward their own destruction. It is not my fault if you listen to me. We all have our own destiny." Following him back to his table, Juno's hips swayed as she walked. Even some of the disinterested patrons in the bar looked up appreciatively as she walked by.

Flipping back her raven black hair, she motioned to the bartender for a drink. "Fortunately for you, Supay, I have come to help." She tapped his nose with her finger before Supay could pull away.

"I doubt that," he said.

"No, really. I figured I'd see how the memory situation was working out. Have you talked to Phoebe lately?"

Supay shook his head. "All she did was e-mail me that she wasn't coming back and was with Apollo."

Juno tsked prettily. "And you bought that? I checked up on the lovebirds. They're keeping house in La Coruna. The lovely Phoebe has most of her memories back, but still isn't with you. Meanwhile, Apollo is wandering around like a lovesick puppy. It is truly disgusting." She leaned back and let Supay take it all in.

Swallowing a gulp of beer, Supay tried to think of what to say. He could not understand. If Phoebe had her memories back, then why was she still with Apollo? What about him? When he did not respond, Juno continued.

"I figured you would have a problem responding. Not to worry, Juno is here to help. I can bring your Phoebe back to you for only a small cost."

Without thinking, Supay nodded. "What is it? And how?"

Juno uncrossed her long, shapely legs. "Well, I have a few spells and tricks still under my sleeve. As long as she is in love with Apollo," Supay flinched, "you will not have a chance of being with her. I could, however, arrange for her to return to being in love with you."

"How?"

Juno leaned forward conspiratorially. "To help you, my friend, I could cast a love spell. She will be in love with you forever, but can never know that you placed the love spell on her."

Supay frowned. "How would she not know? And wouldn't her love be fake?"

Shaking her head, Juno became more serious. "No, it wouldn't. This will only work to remind someone of true love or to jump-start a love that would already be there. I can keep the memory of talking to me and the love spell hidden from her mind reading. There are two catches, however."

Rolling his eyes, Supay waited. Dealing with Juno was dangerous. There were always catches or loopholes to her rules. Seeing that he was not going to say anything, Juno continued. She ticked the issues off her fingers. "Problem one: When I cast the spell, she can never know. If you do tell her or if someone else tells her, the spell will be broken. Once she finds out, she will never be able to love you completely again. She may be in love with you, but she will never be able to reach the peak of true love."

"What will stop you from telling her?" Supay asked.

"My lips are sealed, lovely. I promise not to tell her or a living soul. Not a word will cross my lips."

Supay mulled it over in his mind. "Okay, what is the second catch?"

Juno dimpled cutely. "Why, my payment, of course." She rubbed her leg against his. Glancing around the room, she slipped her toes out of her high heels and pushed her feet up his chair. Stroking him inconspicuously with her foot, she felt him grow hard. Juno smiled wickedly.

"Is your payment what I think it is?" he asked with a slight groan. Considering her normal deals, this could actually be one of the better arrangements.

Juno nodded. Leaning backward, she unbuttoned two additional buttons on her blouse. Unrestrained, her breast pushed outward in an attempt to break free. Supay hesitated. Although he wanted to remain faithful to Phoebe, she was with another man. To have her back, he would have to play Juno's game. He nodded and motioned toward the back of the bar. "Meet me in back. Five minutes."

Juno winked. "Naughty boy."

Walking across the room, she stepped into the bathroom. Within moments, Supay joined her. Shoving her against the wall, he pushed up her skirt. Laughing, she wrapped her legs around him. He struggled with his belt buckle for a moment and then was inside her. Memories of the two or three dates they went on in the past flooded back. He remembered why he had even bothered to date her. She was a devil in disguise in real life, but in bed she was a goddess. Throwing her hands up, her fingertips caught the top of the door. With wild abandon, she worked her hips against his. Supay groaned as his body responded to hers. His mind wanted to hate this, but he could not help it. Her nipples struggled free of their constraints and ran against his body as he ravaged her against the wall. She started to say something and he slapped her.

"Quiet," he growled. "Talking isn't part of your deal." In response, she arched her back and pushed her hips onto him. The movement caused him to become more turned on.

Kissing along his neck, she pulled his hips into hers with her hands. "Hit me," she said. Supay slapped her again. "Harder," she told him. He slapped her harder, and a red mark formed on her face. As he thrust into her again, she bit his shoulder to keep from calling out. Looking at him, she realized a better way to get into his mind. Instead of muffling her screams, she let out a moan. Anyone in the bar would hear and know what passed between them. In moments, someone could walk in and see them against the wall. The thought of someone entering the room was enticing to Supay and Juno. Danger lurked just around the corner, and they were pushing the limits of acceptable human behavior.

Shoving her harder into the door, Supay felt a moment of surprise. He could feel her orgasming around him. He played with her breast as it pressed against him. Every part of her body was opening for him and asking for him to go deeper. With a loud moan, he thrust deeper into her than he ever had before. Right as he started to orgasm, she tightened her muscles around him and drew him even deeper inside. His moan became louder as it mingled with her scream of pleasure.

Pulling out of her body, Supay tried to compose himself and get dressed. His mind and heart were Phoebe's, but all he wanted to do right now was take Juno home and ravage her again. He knew that he'd never want to be with Juno, but he wanted to have her.

Juno straightened her skirt and did not bother to button up her blouse. She did not care about appearances. The only people who would not know they were having sex would have to be deaf. Opening the door, they left the bathroom together and were greeted by the stares of every patron. Supay coughed awkwardly and followed her out of the room.

Walking with Juno to her car, Supay looked around in surprise. "You don't have a vehicle?" he queried.

Juno pointed to a Harley motorcycle. "I don't need one. Care to take a ride with me?"

Supay paused. Animal desires struggled with his love of Phoebe. "I better not. Will the spell start working immediately, or…?"

Shrugging, Juno straddled the bike and pulled on her helmet. The bike fit comfortably between her thighs as it roared to life. Over the sound of the engine, she answered him. "I never can tell with these spells. Either she just realized her love for you, or she will realize it after she sees you again. Good luck and remember—if she finds out about the spell, she will never be able to love you as much."

Nodding, Supay waved her off. It was time to buy a plane ticket.

Chapter Three

Phoebe walked alone again along the seashore. She needed to do something but was not sure what. It was like all of a sudden she realized what her life had become and that she was not supposed to be here. If she was not supposed to be with Apollo, where was she supposed to be? She still needed to tell him that she was pregnant. Over the last few days, she had avoided sleeping with him so that he could not see the tightness that was starting to grow around her abdomen. Thankfully, the morning sickness had stopped. This made it easier for her. She had been trying to walk it off each morning. It had not helped the morning sickness, but walking took her away from Apollo and the possibility that he might notice.

Sitting at her favorite spot by the lighthouse, she heard someone playing bagpipes in the distance. The sound was actually pleasant. Whenever she had listened to the bagpipes on a CD, it had always annoyed her. It made sense that they would sound better outdoors in the open air. Glancing up toward the lighthouse, she saw the outline of a man. For a second, she thought that Apollo had come to search for her. Groaning inwardly, she started to get up as the figure came closer. As the man moved out of the direct sunlight, she made out the dark hair and features of Supay.

Jumping up, she ran over to him and gave him a hug. She had no clue why, but she was excited to see him. It was like she finally found a missing piece. Hugging her back, Supay stepped away. Something was different about her. He paused for a moment and took her appearance in. Her stomach had always been so flat, but now there was a touch of roundness. Phoebe's face had also changed. It was slightly rounder, but almost imperceptibly so. Her entire skin seemed to glow. Supay's eyes widened as he realized what this meant. Inwardly, he cursed his bad luck.

"You and Apollo are having a child." It was not a question.

Phoebe bit her lip. Her hesitation confused him. She stammered out a no before turning red.

"What do you mean 'no'? How could it be otherwise?" His voice sounded harsher than he meant it to, but he could not hide the hurt.

Phoebe shuffled her feet and held up the jade pendant. "The Qilin gave me this and said I would need it. I looked it up after I realized I was pregnant. It is a symbol of fertility."

Supay's eyes opened even wider in surprise. "Wait, so you mean..." he trailed off.

She nodded. "In a couple of months, I will be having your child."

Supay picked her up off the ground and twirled her around in excitement. "That's amazing! Why didn't you tell me? We have to start shopping. The study can be changed into a nursery. Are we having a boy or a girl?"

Phoebe shrugged shyly. "I was thinking it could be a surprise."

Setting her down, Supay stepped back. "This almost made me forget why I was here." Kneeling on one knee, he took out a small velvet box. Nervously, he opened it and held out the diamond ring inside.

"Phoebe, I know that the last few months have been confusing. All I wanted to do was be with you, but I couldn't find where you went. You are my soul mate and the person that I am supposed to spend the rest of my life with. Now that your memories are returning, I was hoping that you would still feel the same way about me. Phoebe, will you marry me?" He waited for what seemed like a lifetime for her to respond.

Holding the ring in her hand, Phoebe waited for her mind to come up with an answer. After all of the confusion and stress of the last few months, this seemed right. She would have to break it off with Apollo, but that was expected. Apollo had known that this might happen. As her memories returned, she even felt at times like he had taken advantage of her memory loss. He had tried to change her life to what he wanted it to be instead of what it was supposed to be. Looking up at Supay, Phoebe nodded. "Yes, I will marry you."

Standing up, Supay wrapped his arms around her in a passionate embrace. She tipped her head back for him to kiss her. In that moment, it was like nothing had ever changed. They were together again and everything felt right. Arm in arm, they walked together along the beach. From time to time, Supay would place his hand on her stomach to see if the baby would kick.

In the distance, Apollo had left the condo to find Phoebe. She had not arrived on time for dinner, and he was worried that something might have happened. Strolling confidently along the beach, he reached her favorite spot. She was not there. Confused, he started to walk past the spot. The remaining portion of beach was a favorite of locals and tourists. Filled with soft white sand, the spot was perfect for sun bathing. As he walked across the beach, Apollo caught sight of Phoebe and Supay. Cursing slightly, he took a step back to see what was going on.

In front of him, Phoebe was laughing as she stepped out of a swimsuit cover-up. She looked happier than he had seen her for weeks. Supay was applying sun block on her back. Apollo watched as Supay made her lie back so he could apply it to her stomach. As Supay kissed her belly button, Apollo realized what he had missed for the last few months. Phoebe was pregnant. The only reason she would not have told him was if... the thought trailed off in his mind.

Turning away, he walked back to the condo. He poured a glass of whiskey and tossed it back. Pouring another glass, he grabbed a backpack and put all of his must-have items into it. If she wanted to be with Supay, Apollo had no reason to hang around. Throwing everything in the backpack, he tipped back another glass of whiskey. He wrote a note and placed it on the fridge before giving a last glance at everything around him. It was nice while it lasted, but it looked like this dream was over for him.

Hours later, Phoebe quietly opened the door to the condo. It was time for her to face Apollo. She had asked Supay to stay behind so she could break the news gently to him. Entering the condo, she noticed the empty whiskey bottle on the table. Dinner had never been made. Worried, she went into their bedroom and realized that he was gone. Phoebe sat down on the bed and started to cry. She had wanted to explain and help him to understand. How could he possibly forgive her if she could not even see him? Drying her tears, she went to the kitchen to grab a quick snack before leaving. On the fridge, a note was left. Scrawled across were the words "I know" and nothing else. Sighing, Phoebe pulled the note down and returned to the room to pack her bags. Someday, she would explain. Until Apollo had healed some more, it did not look like explaining would be possible.

Leaving the condo, she dialed Supay's number on her phone. Within minutes, he arrived at the ground floor of the condo and was waiting for her. Helping with her bags, Supay did not want to pry into how the conversation went. Instead, he kissed her gently on the lips and opened her car door. In a few short hours, they would be back to Peru and preparing for the birth of their first child. Everything was working out perfectly. It had taken him over a year, but his life was finally returning to a semblance of order.

-To be continued in Book 5-

If you enjoyed this title, I would appreciate your leaving a review of the book. Good reviews encourage an author to write as well as help books to sell. Good reviews can be just a few short sentences describing what you liked about the book without having a spoiler. If you could spend 30 seconds writing a review, I would appreciate it: you can review this title right now at your favorite retailer.

Here is a preview of the **next story** you may enjoy:

Exposed - The Daemon Paranormal Romance Chronicles, Book 5

IN PERU, Supay and Phoebe had just welcomed their daughter into the world. The tiny infant was named Irene. To the outside world, the little family seemed like a nexus of harmony. Few outsiders would realize the number of troubles they had gone through in the last few years.

It had all started when Phoebe was approached by Apollo. Raised in foster care, she never knew that she was a daemon. Until that day, Phoebe had made all of her money by telling fortunes. As a daemon, she had a unique talent—her ability was to read people's minds and see what their innermost thoughts were. When Apollo showed up, he needed help finding the Qilin. According to the prophecy, the Qilin would indicate the next great leader or wise man. Apollo had drawn her into the hunt because the Qilin was going under a different name, and he needed someone to read minds in order to find her. Together, they had quickly located the Qilin and started a passionate romance. Before long, it ended. Phoebe discovered at the death of the Qilin that Apollo's talent was to give suggestions or manipulate the minds of other people. Due to this, Phoebe could never truly trust him. She could not be certain that her love for him was not just another manipulation. At the same time, she discovered that her dog was actually a shape shifter known as Supay. Although she had felt betrayed at first, she came to terms with this oddity over time. Supay had become her dog so that he could protect her and hopefully save the

Qilin. Although it had not helped the Qilin, his protection had kept her safe.

Phoebe picked up Irene and sat down in the rocking chair. It was so peaceful in the nursery. Before long, Supay would return home. Although the infighting among the daemons had died down, it still caused problems. Supay had been stretched to the maximum of his abilities as he tried to bring peace. Their desire to bring peace had come at a temporary cost; the meddlesome siren, Juno, had agreed to stop causing arguments and fighting among the daemons, provided Phoebe give up her memories. Although Phoebe eventually got those memories back, it had led to a temporary break from Juno.

As Irene fell asleep, Phoebe walked into the living room. She started to sit down when Supay walked in. He immediately came up to her for a kiss.

"How are my lovely ladies today?" he asked. Phoebe held him closer and kissed him back hungrily.

"The little one is fine, but the older one needs some attention," she teased. Supay held her closer. Her scent was enticing. Everywhere he turned in his apartment, he could smell her. Running his fingers through her hair, he pulled her head back for another kiss. The ferocity of her passion surprised him and made him want more. Setting his things down, he looked at her inquisitively. Slowly, he started to unbutton his jacket and waited for her to respond. When she started to pull off her shirt as well, he was certain. She wanted him.

Quietly, they slipped off their clothes and sank to the floor. Like secret trysts among teenagers, they had to remain quiet and not wake up Irene. Running his finger down her naked body, Supay started to play with her clit. He slipped his fingers inside of her and realized how wet she was.

"Mmm... you know, we could try putting that jade necklace on again," he teased. Reaching onto the table, he wrapped the necklace around her neck. Given to her by the Qilin, it was the only reason she could even have children with him. Without the aid of the fertility talisman, she would never have been able to have children outside of her daemon family.

If you enjoyed this sample then look for **Exposed - The Daemon Paranormal Romance Chronicles, Book 5**.

Here is a preview of **another story** you may also enjoy:

JARED WAS quiet for the next few hours as they continued their drive. He hadn't responded when Ananda explained that she had seen his sister and the message she had given her. The idea that not only had Sophie known about her brother's gift but somehow also had the gift herself was alarming and Ananda just knew that asking questions now would be a bad move. So rather than talk and risk upsetting the man further, Ananda decided to catch up on as much sleep as possible. She was still unsure of their destination and secretly she was terrified that the dark figure from her vision would find them before they reached whatever destination they were heading to.

"I'm sorry." The sound of Jared's voice was almost overly loud in the quiet of the car. Ananda opened her eyes but refused to turn around. Somehow she knew that whatever the man needed to say, it would be much easier for him to get it out if she weren't looking at him. "I'm not angry with you…it's just…" Jared paused, as if to gather courage. "The whole time we were growing up, Sophie never ever told me she had a gift. Not even when I started hearing voices and told her. I always thought that if I had done more, I could have saved her that day. If only I had told someone about Kevin instead of hiding away like a coward. Or if I had stayed in the cafeteria that day…"

"Then you would have died along with everyone else and you wouldn't have been here, now, alive and able to keep me from being caught or killed by whoever is after me!" Ananda couldn't help but turn to look at the man. The sound of his grief was almost more than she could bear. "I didn't know your sister, but I'm sure she would never have wanted you to be there that day. She was your big sister and for some reason, for some reason that I just can't explain, I know she knew what was going to happen."

If not for his iron grip on the steering wheel, Jared might have jerked out of his chair with shock. "What?" He couldn't wrap his head around the thought. Even if Sophie had had the gift, she wasn't old enough for extra abilities to have manifested. "She wasn't old enough to have that ability. Abilities like that don't manifest until after maturation."

"I know, I know you said that but…I don't know how to explain it Jared." She put her hand softly on Jared's shoulder, willing him to understand what she saw and felt. Suddenly a tingling sensation manifested almost like an itch behind her ear. The feeling traveled down her arm and into the tips of her fingers as they rested against Jared's warm skin until she was sure that the man had to be feeling something. It was odd how surely Ananda felt about Jared when they had only met one another seventy-two hours ago. She spared a thought for Kerri and wondered what her dearest friend was doing in her absence. "Do you think I could call Kerri, or my parents? I mean, would it be safe to call them? They aren't in any danger right?"

If you enjoyed this sample then look for **Revealed - The Mind Talker Paranormal Romance Series, Book 4**.

Other Books by Darla Dunbar

- The Romeo Alpha BBW Paranormal Shifter Romance Series

- Romeo Alpha Blood Lines Romance

- The Alpha Feud BBW Paranormal Shifter Romance Series

- The Alpha Packed BBW Paranormal Shifter Romance Series

- The Mind Talker Paranormal Romance Series

- The Leather Satchel Paranormal Romance Series

Get the latest update on new releases from the author at:

https://darladunbar.com/newsletter/

About the Author - Darla Dunbar

Darla has been interested in paranormal romance since she was a teenager in high school. It was then that she discovered she could fulfill her fantasies through her writing.

Observing people and human behavior in the area of romance has always been one of her favorite pastimes. Combining that with an overactive imagination is a sure fire way of coming up with interesting themes.

Connect with Darla Dunbar

I really appreciate you reading my book! Here are my social media coordinates:

Friend me on Facebook:
https://www.facebook.com/darladunbar/

Follow me on Twitter: https://twitter.com/DarlDunbar

Check me out on Goodreads:
https://www.goodreads.com/author/show/8425857.Darl
a_Dunbar

Subscribe to my newsletter:
https://darladunbar.com/newsletter/

Visit my website: https://darladunbar.com/